# Zero Hour

## by Jim Brochu

A SAMUEL FRENCH ACTING EDITION

SAMUEL FRENCH

FOUNDED 1830

NEW YORK HOLLYWOOD LONDON TORONTO

SAMUELFRENCH.COM

## MUSIC USE NOTE



## IMPORTANT BILLING AND CREDIT
## REQUIREMENTS

*ZERO HOUR* was first produced by the West Coast Jewish Theatre at the Egyptian Studio Theatre in Los Angeles, California on July 6, 2006.

*ZERO HOUR* opened Off-Broadway on November 22, 2009 at Theatre at St. Clement's, 423 West 46th Street, New York City. It was produced by Kurt Peterson, Edmund Gaynes and the Peccadillo Theater Company (Kevin Kennedy and Dan Wackerman); Associate Producer, Richard I. Bloch. The production was directed by Piper Laurie. Production assistant, Julia Beardsley. Production Stage Manager was Donald William Myers. The Assistant Stage Manager was Jeramiah Peay. The set design was by Josh Iacovelli. The lighting design was by Jason Arnold. Marketing was by Leanne Schanzer and Associates and the General Press Representative was David Gersten and Associates. General Management was by Jessimeg Productions. Logo by Gymbreaux, Graphics and Design by Frank Dain. Artistic Associate, Steve Schalchlin. The original production starred Jim Brochu as The Artist.

# AUTHOR'S NOTES

It was 1962. I was a sophomore in high school, enamored with the theatre and lucky enough to have a mentor named David Burns. Davy was co-starring with Zero in *A Funny Thing Happened on the Way to the Forum*. I had no idea who Zero Mostel was when I first saw the show but was knocked out by the comedic force of nature that ruled over the stage of the Alvin Theatre.

I made my way backstage to see Davy and literally ran into Mostel who looked like he had just taken a shower in his costume – steamy and covered with sweat. I was attending military school and dressed in my West Point style uniform which caught his attention. "You must be General Nuisance. What do you want?" he snorted.

"I'm here to see Davy Burns," I said.

"You never come to see me!" he grunted as he brushed past me and disappeared down the dark hallway

The next week, I saw the show again, visited Davy and then went to Zero's dressing room. He was reading the riot act to one of the actors who he thought had upstaged him. The funny man I loved onstage had become a screaming maniac and all I could do was stand back and cringe. The actor apologized and left. Zero looked at me with exploding eyes and said, "What do you want?"

"To say hello," I managed to articulate.

His rage turned to total charm in a nanosecond.

"Well, hello! Come in."

I sat in his dressing room as he asked me all sorts of questions - like why was I a fat kid in a military uniform? From that night until he left the show, whenever I came to visit Davy, I always spent time with Zero too.

On the second night of *Fiddler on the Roof*, I flew to New York from Pittsburgh, where I was studying drama at Carnegie Tech. I sat in the first row of the Imperial Theatre and was dazzled by the uplifting, heartbreaking performance that unfolded just a few feet away from me. I knew from *Forum* that Zero was a master comedian, but I didn't know until *Fiddler* that he was a towering dramatic actor. He waved to me at the bows and I felt as though I had been knighted.

Still drenched with sweat, he welcomed me into his dressing room like an old friend. I was so moved by his performance I found it difficult to talk.

A few years later, when I had become a professional actor, I ran into Zero on the street and asked him for an autographed picture of himself. He screamed at me, "You're not worthy!" and went on his way. I was shocked - yet not shocked - because his behavior was as outrageous offstage as it was on.

But he did accept an invitation to come see my off-Broadway debut in a show called *Unfair To Goliath.* The day after he attended, I found a manila envelope on my dressing table. Inside was an autographed picture of Zero signed, "To Jimmy, with my admiration, Zero…"

Years later, I looked at that picture when I heard of his death and hoped that someday I could give back to Zero something of what he gave to me. *Zero Hour* is a tribute to the life of a man who overcame both physical and social obstacles to become one of most enduring giants in the history of the American Theatre. This play is for you, Zero – with *my* admiration.

*–Jim Brochu*

## THE CHARACTER

The Artist – Male

## THE TIME

July, 1977. Late afternoon.

## THE PLACE

New York City.
A painter's loft on the top floor of 51 West 28th Street.

*This play is dedicated to Sammy M., Davy B., Lou J.,*
*Jack G., Jack A., and always…*
*for Steve.*

*Special thanks to Jerry Bock and Sheldon Harnick.*

# ACT ONE

*(AT RISE: With the feel of a rundown tenement, it looks as though the room has been ransacked but no, that's the way* **THE ARTIST** *likes it.)*

*(A pre-war building, [World War I, that is] naked brick walls and brown plaster lend a sepia-tone to the room and yet shafts of light punctuate the darkness through an upstage left skylight.)*

*(Under the skylight is a large, old paint-splattered easel that is embracing another of the many "works in progress." A kitchen chair faces it and a small work table sits just to the left of it.)*

*(There are two doors. The upstage right door is a closet, while the larger upstage left door leads to a toilet.)*

*(A coat rack stands just to the left of the door and is laden with a selection of caps, coats, smocks and a black, silver tipped walking stick that is hung there with uncharacteristic care.)*

*(There are dozens of finished and half-finished canvases of all sizes dotting the wall and the room, along with sculptures, tubes of paint and blank canvases. There is a well-used yet enormously comfortable upholstered chair hovering near stage right - a shawl thrown over it to pep up its antiquity.)*

*(Old newspapers and various incongruous objects — a typewriter, hot water bottle, stacks of old newspapers punctuate the room. The walls of the studio can be more suggestive than real, more impressionist than detailed.)*

*As the lights come up,* **THE ARTIST** *is sitting at the easel, his back to the audience, brush in hand, flaying away at the canvas, totally absorbed in the act of creation.)*

*(There is a knock at an unseen door.)*

*(The* **ARTIST** *keeps painting.)*

**THE ARTIST.** Go away!

*(another knock)*

Go away or I'll call the police.

*(another knock)*

Go away or I shall unleash the dogs.

*(He barks a few times.)*

Back! Back! There's plague here!

*(Another knock. More determined.)*

All right then....

*(The* **ARTIST** *stands, turns and faces his inquisitor.)*

What are you standing outside for? Come in!

*(A beat)*

Well, there you are! You're the reporter, right? You're not what I expected. Well, I always expect a newspaper man to look bookish. You don't look bookish. In fact, you look rather distinguished like a Jewish goyishe Woody Allen. Come in.

*(All smiles)*

Come in. Welcome to my sanctuary, my studio, my world apart. You got here right on time. In fact, you're five minutes early. I hate people who come on time. And I hate them more if they come five minutes early. It means you are bereft of individuality. You have an inferiority complex but you're on an ego trip; a sheep in the flock who likes to stand out. A mass of contradictions – the polite kind that says please and thank you but you don't mean it. Quick! Close the door behind you; you're letting the flies out!

So what's this interview for anyway, putz?

*(a beat)*

Why do I call you putz? I call you putz because I don't know your name. No, I don't want to know your name. This is an interview, it's not a relationship. What? Well, I'm sorry. I didn't mean to offend you. I apologize. It was a slip of the tongue. You must forgive me. I've been traveling and I'm exhausted. I promise I won't call you putz.

So, schmuck! What is this interview for anyway? The *New York Times?* All the news that's fit to print? That's what we used to say about the great artist, Goya – all the nudes that are fit to paint.

*(He makes himself laugh. The interviewer is not responding.)*

I see you've had a humor bypass. Why am I exhausted? Because I just got back from London a few hours ago. London! God, that's going to be a beautiful city when it's finished. I was there doing "The Muppet Show." Do you know, Kermit the Frog and Miss Piggy are the two greatest actors I ever worked with and if you get into an argument, you can always use them to wash your car. I haven't even been home yet. I had to get a fix. To get some paint on my hands. Now take that stool and sit.

*(sizing up his model)*

Now that's amazing. You look shorter when you're standing up. You sit down you look rather tall and then you stand up and you were shorter than you were sitting down. I've never seen anything like it. Now loosen your tie a little and move into the light. You see it's all about the light, my dear friend. Shadow and highlight. It's what painting is all about. It's what life is all about. But to tell you the truth – that jacket doesn't look good in any light. Jesus, it's ugly. Okay, now move in a little bit....

What am I doing? I'm making you my model...I don't care if you've never been a model before. It's not exactly skilled labor. You turn this way, you turn that way. You do as you're told. Now turn to your left. Oh, but you're from *The New York Times*. How much further left can you turn?

Okay, ask a question. Tell you a secret? That's a stupid question. I have no secrets. My life is an open zipper. Now ask a real question...my real first name? It's Gwendolyn!

Put your notes down. Didn't you do your homework? Find out all about me before you got here? Good! What year was I born? Correct, I was born in 1915...It was a very good year.

I remember every minute of it: Wilson kept us out of war, the Lusitania sank, it cost two cents to send a letter from New York City all the way to California. Two cents! Of course it didn't get there until 1922 – and I was born on a beautiful farm out in the middle of the country. Yes I was. It was a small radish farm near the intersection of Kings Highway and Pitkin Avenue. The Jews who settled there came from Eastern Europe and they loved to live and work the land and there was a lot of farmland in Brooklyn back then that wasn't Prospect Park and all covered with concrete.

*(He sits in his big chair and enjoys his reverie.)*

*(The light change to envelop him in the spirit of his childhood. The voice of a woman singing a Jewish lullaby is heard far off in the past.)*

Both my parents were from Austria. Vienna. My mother was so...little. Her name was Cina. Cina Druchs. But when she came to America, everyone called her Celia. My father had been married before her. His first wife died, left him with four children. But my mother loved them like they were her very own and then had four more. My father, Israel Mostel, was a sidewalk rabbi. Meaning he wasn't really a rabbi but people treated him like one. He was a wise and gentle man. A learned man – a man who kept the family together the best way he knew how making a living as a wine chemist. And then he ran a kosher slaughter-house after we moved to Connecticut – to the busting metropolis of Moodus where there was one shepherd and twelve very nervous sheep.

Acres of rolling hills – thousands of trees. It was unnatural. You know how most people in the city save their money to move to the country? For us, it was the other way around. We saved our money so we could move back to a tenement because Mama wanted to expose us to culture. To the arts.

All of us in two rooms. So crowded...but so happy. It was crazy. All of us - Mama, Papa, my five brothers, two sisters and me all clamoring to be the center of attention. I wanted to be the center of attention more than any of them. But Mama was so happy to be back in the city where there were concert halls and museums. Almost every day when I was a child, she would dress me in a black velvet suit and take me to the Metropolitan Museum of Art where I would sit for hours copying the great masters and she would stand behind me watching and to any visitor passing by she would tell them, "Der ist mein sohn der Kunstler."

When I was nine years old, I drew a picture of my father. I showed it to my mother. She said, "Look, he's nine years old and he paints like a man." Then when I was twenty I did an abstract and showed it to her. She said, "Look, he's twenty years old and he paints like a child." My mother always understood my need to paint, this compulsion! But never my father. He said it was against our religion to create a graven image. But it's not a graven image, papa. It's not betraying my faith to paint a picture. Any more than to marry the person I loved. I wanted to tell you. I wanted you to understand. About everything. I tried to get to you, papa.

*(It seems he's going a little nuts.)*

They wouldn't let me in to see you. They tried to kill me. My own brothers – they tried to kill me.

*(The lights restore as he snaps out of his daydream.)*

What? What was I talking about? What do you mean you don't remember? I was talking about my father. Did you know my father had the only wine license in New York City during prohibition? He could have made a fortune for the family if he made it for the bootleggers. But he wouldn't do it. He only made sacramental wine. Money was never important to him. We had enough.

*(The phone rings.)*

There was a time my father...

*(The phone rings again. He gets up to answer it.)*

You can relax for a minute.

*(He keeps staring at the interviewer as he crosses, then...)*

Did you pick out that jacket during a total eclipse? It's the ugliest thing I've ever seen.

*(He answers the phone.)*

Palestinian Anti-Defamation League. This is Yassir speaking.

*(A beat)*

This is a recorded message so stop talking. Who? How dare you. How many times do I have to tell you never to call me here? This is my sanctuary! My studio. I don't care. You have violated me. You have desecrated my art! How did you get this number? What do you want? And you called me for that? You interrupted my work for that!

*(screams into the receiver:)*

May I ask you a question? How do you sleep at night?

*(He slams the phone down. A long beat as he returns to the drawing table.)*

My wife. She needs a pint of sour cream. Remind me to have this number changed. No, I'm serious. Do you know when Kate and I got married...what – thirty-three years ago? – She thought that I was going to give up my painting, this studio – She thought it was a hobby – just someplace to pass the time. I think she thought I had a broad down here. She didn't realize painting is my life.

Kate is short for Kathryn. Kathryn Harkin. She came from the original dysfunctional family. That's why she fell in love with me. I was a dysfunctional family all by myself.

What a pair – a dysfunctional Catholic Rockette from Philadelphia and a dysfunctional Jewish painter from New York. When we first met, I was afraid that being a Jew, I was going to scare her off and I thought I'll never have a chance with a woman as beautiful as this is in my life. So I lied to her. I told her my real name was Remo Ferrugia and that my parents were from Tuscany and that my great uncle was Pope Leo XIII. My mother overheard me talking to her on the phone one day and was shocked to find out that her father's uncle from Minsk turned out to be the head of the Roman Catholic Church.

*(changing the mood)*

Kate was wonderful but then there was Kate's mother. She was…oh, what's the word for it…oh yes, CRAZY! The only smart thing that mishugenah woman ever did was to force Kate to have dancing lessons when she was a little girl. And…when Kate was a little girl, her mother fell down in a department store and so she sued the store and they settled with her for five hundred dollars. Whenever the family needed money, her mother went out and fell down.

When Kate and I first started going out together, her mother invited us to dinner. It was her way of sizing me up. And Kate explained to her all about my being Jewish and kosher and keeping meat and dairy separate. So that night her mother served us a beautiful dinner – roast loin of pork - Alfredo. You know what they say, recipes speak louder than words. And Jewish dietary laws are very strict – pork and shellfish may only be eaten in Chinese restaurants. Her mother asked why I didn't eat anything. I told her I had matzoh poisoning.

When Kate and I first got married, her mother dropped in for a little visit one day and stayed for five years. FIVE YEARS! In those five years she lived with us, we spoke eighteen words to each other – nine of them were "fuck" and the other nine were "you." Crazy. Life is crazy. But Kate still wanted me to give up painting and if I hadn't have had my art, we never would have met.

That's right, we met at Café Society. I could tell you did your homework. But, don't you see? One thing leads to another. I studied art at CCNY, from CCNY they asked me to go give lectures on art at Union Halls, my lectures were filled with jokes, the jokes led me to benefits, the benefits led me to nightclubs and the nightclubs led me to the greatest nightclub of them all - Café Society. Two Sheridan Square. And the greatest salary of them all. Four hundred dollars a week. Back then? That was a fortune!

*(He puts down the paintbrush as he moves away from the drawing table. lights change, bringing us back to the musky cellar nightclub. Music of a jazz trio starts under...)*

The first night I was there – December 28, 1941, Barney Josephson, the owner, met me outside. He walked me down the stairs into the back of the club and there was a girl singer on the stage. There wasn't a sound in the room except for that voice. Usually there's a buzz – a couple of loudmouth drunks at the bar – people talking, you know – hell, it's a nightclub. But that night that voice had mesmerized three hundred people.

*(We hear the woman's voice singing a song.)*

And I had to follow her. I said to Barney, "Who is that?" He told me. And all I could think of was, "How do you follow Billie Holiday? Especially when you're doing an imitation of a teapot."

*(Applause. He moves to the other side of the stage as the lights crossfade.)*

Then I was backstage standing next to Ivan Black. He was the press agent for the club. The emcee said, "Now welcome the brightest new star on the comedy horizon - Zero Mostel!" And I thought, "Who the hell is that?" "Why didn't he say Sammy Mostel? My name is Sam. Who changed my name?" Ivan Black said, "I changed it. That's your new name." I said, "I don't need a new name. My name is Sam. And why Zero?" Ivan said, "Do you remember what you told me your grade school average was? And besides, you started from nothing." I thought, "Well, it's too late now" so out I went.

*(Crossing to centerstage, he steps into a spotlight.)*

Good evening Ladies and Gentlemen. I just heard a remarkable story I wanted to share with you. It seems an Chassidic Rabbi walked into a bar. The rabbi had a parrot on his shoulder. The bartender said, "Where did you get that?" The parrot said, "They're all over Brooklyn." They laughed. I did my imitation of a teapot.

*(He puts both his hands on his hips making two "handles," looks at them with a twinkle in his eye and sings the first lines of "The Teapot" song…*)*

*(He notices he has two handles)*

Fuck! I'm a sugar bowl!  I did my imitation of a butterfly at rest…

*(He does it.)*

…and they laughed again. People came to see me. And then one night Kate was right there.

*(The lights restore to "the studio.")*

She was with my old friend Phil Loeb. That's right. Phil Loeb from *The Goldbergs*. You did do your homework. No. I don't talk about Phil. Too depressing. I'll just say he was there with Kate. Dear Kate. Beautiful Kate. Pain in the ass, Kate.  God, she was the perfect woman. Beautiful, funny, intellectual, interested in everything, wanting to live, wanting to love. Wanting to marry me. There was only one problem. I was already married. To a Schverd. No, that's not a Yiddish term - that was her name - Clara Schverd. We grew up together. Went to school together. I carried her books. We were horny Jewish kids. So back then, horny Jewish kids got married. I chased her until I caught her and then she didn't want me anymore. Clara had the sense of humor of a grapefruit. Nothing I did could make her laugh. Until I took my clothes off. Then she laughed.

But Kate was different. Kate had the face of a Rockette. Clara had the face of a rock. Kate thought I was the funniest man in the world. She laughed at everything I said. And Kate had a great laugh – it was a low, rumbling, genuine laugh – like the sound a dog makes just before it throws up.  And I didn't have to take my clothes off.

Finally, after a year Clara agreed to a divorce for $5,000 cash and fifty percent of my salary for the next two years – so I gave her the $5,000 cash and joined the army. But I was free of her. Free of the Schverd forever!

*(answering a question)*

I only lasted in the army for six months. They hook me up to the USO. They sent me to Europe. I entertained the troops. Then I developed an ulcer. They sent me to the Army doctor. I walked in for my appointment. I said, "Well, doctor?" The doctor said, "You must stop masturbating!" I said, "Why, doctor?" He said, "Because I'm trying to examine you!" He said, He told me I had a spastic colon. I told him he had a spastic brain. He said, "I'm going to cure you of this right now." I said, "How are you going to do that?" He said, "I'm going to give you a coffee enema." I said, "You're what?" Then he ordered me to bend over the table. He took the coffee and applied it. I screamed. The doctor said, "Too hot?" I said, "No, too sweet!" I was discharged that afternoon. What do you mean that's not what you heard?

My politics? My politics had nothing to do with my discharge. Sure I was a liberal. I was even a Marxist. Anybody with a half a brain was. Because of what was going on in Europe. Fascism! Hitler! Socialists weren't fighting America. We were fighting Fascism. Nobody ever thought that America would embrace a socialist way of life - but we all thought the government could help out a little.

And so did Franklin Delano Roosevelt - one of the greatest Jewish minds in the history of the world. A poor man's mentality in rich man's clothing. He gave us social security – not socialist security - and the Works Progress Administration.

And did the beneficiaries of said administration create an overthrow of the government? No, they created timeless works of art. They gave us Clifford Odets and Elmer Rice and Harold Clurman and John Houseman and Orson Welles and - although we could have done without Houseman – what a pain in the ass he was – but they gave us WORK! When nobody else had the means to give us work.

The government gave me canvas and brush and paint and they gave it to Rockwell Kent and Jackson Pollack, Moses Soyer and Diego Rivera. Think about the great works of art that would have remained unpainted… the great dramas that would have remained unwritten. Think about a world without *Awake and Sing* and *Street Scene.* Without Bertholt Brecht, without Kurt Weill. It would have been a national tragedy. Like your jacket. God, it is awful. I came home from the army, and Katie and I got married

How did my parents accept the new marriage? Well, they knew I wasn't a religious Jew. So when they heard I had married Kate, they refused to meet her, declared me dead, covered the mirrors, sat shivah for a week and threatened to commit suicide. Other than that, they took it very well. If only Kate's mother could have done the same thing. But Kate did change my life - she turned me into an actor!

I was doing a revue with Imogene Coca and "Loose Lips" - that's Jerome Robbins. Jerry and I have a love-hate relationship. He had a love hate relationship with everyone. Including himself. Anyway, I was doing my night club act and "Loose Lips" says to me that he thinks I would be a very good actor and I should study. Study what? The reviews for the show were terrible. Especially for me. One critic said, "Zero lives up to his name."

One night after the show I was suppose to go right home. I was walking up 34th Street. By the way, we had the greatest apartment in New York City – on 46th street between 5th and 6th Avenue. Huge rooms with high ceilings and an elevator that opened right into the living room. The first time Kate's mother came to visit us there, the elevator door opened, she walked in, she thought we were living in a department store. She thought she had walked into the furniture section.

*(a beat)*

So she fell down and asked us for five hundred dollars.

People would just stop by anytime. It was wonderful. We'd hear the elevator and you never knew who was going to walk through those doors. Great painters, great actors, bad actors, musicians, FBI men.

But that's another story. Where was I? Right, walking up 34th Street. Kate was studying acting. I thought she was wasting her time and my money. I found myself walking past her class and thought I'd go in and make fun of her and then walk her home. But it was interesting. And she was very good. He wasn't teaching her how to act. He was teaching her techniques – some tricks. I was using characters in my nightclub act, so I thought maybe he could teach me a few tricks to keep them fresh. I said, "Give me a lesson." He said, "Have you studied the classics?" I told him, "Of course I studied the classics." He asked me, "Where did you study the classics?" I told him, "Grossingers". He said, "Get up on the stage and do something". I said, "You're the teacher, you do something!" He said, "Improvise!" So I improvised.

*(He picks up a paintbrush and uses it as a telephone, making a plan. As he talks, the lights change to support the mood.)*

"Hello, Harry. Harry's it's me Max. Harry, stop talking. Shut up and listen. I know I owe you money, Harry. I'm late with my payment. Yes, I know that too. I know to the penny how much I owe you and you're going to get it back. You're going to get in back in one month in one lump sum and I'm going to give you a hundred dollars more than I owe you. It's none of your business where I'm going to get the money. Just don't worry; you're going to get yours."

*(puts down the fake phone)*

It's none of your business. That's funny. It's my business. This business I hate. This business that's chained me down for thirty years.

*(He mimes picking up gasoline cans and throwing fuel around the room.)*

And now it's all going to go up in smoke. A beautiful black cloud of smoke that will carry my debts and woes to the sky and forever relieve me of this burden of my business. I'll only be collecting my own money anyway. Years of paying insurance premiums. I've put more into the premiums than I'm going to be taking out. Enough to live for the rest of my life. To care for my wife and to give my son the life I've never had. A good home, not the shack we live in now. And a fine education. He'll be a professional man. A doctor. A lawyer. Somebody. Somebody to look up to. Someone to be proud of. A bright shinning light!

*(He mimes throwing the match on the building and runs to the other side of the stage to watch, yelling as he goes.)*

BURN!!! That's right! Burn, baby, burn! All my problems going up in smoke! Burn, baby, burn. No more responsibility. Burn, baby, burn. Call up the van and move me to Easy Street.

*(sees his wife coming.)*

My wife. I have to pretend I'm upset. I want her to think it's an accident. Stella, darling. Calm down, it's going to be alright. It couldn't be helped. Don't cry, darling. Of course I called the fire department. I'm sure they're on their way. Stella, don't cry. You mustn't be so upset. I'm safe. It's only a building. What do you mean, "Where's little Herbie?" He was home with you. What? You put him in the back room to take a nap? What do you mean did I see him come out? No, I didn't see him come out. He's still in there.

*(horrified, he screams)*

HE'S STILL IN THERE. My baby is burning. NOOOOOOOOOO!

*(The lights restore. An instant, complete change of mood.)*

Then I said to the teacher - "Now, do you want it see it funny?" So I did it funny. I ran into the building, saved the kid, sewed him back together and we all lived happily ever after.

So Kate and I studied acting together. She made me better. Then the phone rang. The man said he was Louis B. Meyer. I thought it was a joke. I thought it was Sam Jaffe. But it was Louis B. Mayer. He signed me to a seven year contract. He brought me out to star in *Du Barry Was A Lady* with Lucille Ball. Beautiful and funny.

I was in Hollywood to be an actor. So what did he want me to do? My night club act. After the first day of shooting, Meyer calls me, he says…

*(as Meyer)*

"Mostel, I'm having a party at my house next Saturday night for the heads of every major motion picture studio in town – every A list star and I want you there."

*(as himself)*

Well, thank you, Mr. Meyer.

*(as Meyer)*

"And you're going to be the entertainment. I'm going to show you off because you're my boy. I want your best material. Seven-thirty. Saturday night. Use the back door and don't be late."

*(as himself again)*

I wasn't late. I didn't go. I went to Long Beach to do a benefit for the Longshoreman's Union. Eleanor Roosevelt was there. I gave her her first blintz. And with those teeth.

That was on a Saturday. On Monday I was on my way back to New York with most of my act on the cutting room floor. I didn't mind. I was going home to my beautiful Katie and that great apartment. We were living in the lap of luxury, but unfortunately, you never know when luxury is going to stand up.

Remember I told you how the elevator opened into our apartment. It was never locked. We loved people to come over. Some of the greatest thinkers in the world got into some of the most thought provoking and stimulating debates right in our living room. People would go across the country to hear these people speak and we didn't even have to put our shoes on.

And then one day, the elevator opened and two men walked in. Two strangers. We greeted them very warmly. They stared at us. We asked them if they had the right apartment. They did. We asked them what they wanted. They stared some more. We weren't afraid of them; they were too dull to be threatening. We knew they weren't in the theatre, they were wearing ties. I didn't want them to feel uncomfortable so I put a few ties on over my pajamas. They had the gall to tell us they were looking for an apartment and had heard that we knew everything about the neighborhood. Oh, and if we didn't know of an apartment, maybe we knew where there was a communist party meeting. I told them I had no idea. I wasn't a communist. And I didn't know of any. They kept looking around the place, still pretending they weren't G-Men. I asked them if they wanted a piece of fruit or perhaps a glass of lemonade. Through a suspicious squint, one of them said, "That's very generous of you." I said, "Well, as Trotsky used to say, 'Share and share alike.'"

After what seemed liked fourteen hours of silence I finally herded them back on the elevator and as just as the door closed I said, "Goodbye gentlemen…AND J. EDGAR HOOVER WEARS A DRESS!" Two years ago, we found out I was right.

After those two men left, the elevator doors didn't open as often. People who were my friends crossed the street if they saw me coming so they didn't have to say hello. The phone stopped ringing. The checks stopped coming. The government that once gave me paint now gave me paranoia.

You wanted to know a secret? I got one. I'm the stupidest man that ever lived.

One night, I'm in a bar having a drink with an actor friend and he says, "Zee, I'm so miserable. I'm not working. I don't know why." I said, "Hey, I'm not working, either". And he says to me, "Well, you're blacklisted."

The blacklist. No, we have to talk about it. If we don't then it will happen all over again. We'll be governed by fear. That can't happen. We have to remember what happened to people like me. To Burgess Meredith. To Anne Revere. Jack Gilford. And then there was the other side. The ones who gave names – like Elia Kazan. He gave them names. And Lee J. Cobb. He gave them names. And Jerome Rabinowitz – Jerry Robbins - he gave them names.

They called Robbins to testify in 1953. He had to go home twice to change his underwear before he got to the hearings he was so terrified. But then he kissed the feet of the committee; said he was at a party meeting in 1947 with Lionel Berman and Jerry Chodorov and Madeline Lee who was married to Jack Gilford. Brilliant Madeline, dear Madeline, frightening Madeline, the red menace – a radio actress who made baby noises for a living.

He gave them the names of my friends. And the thing about Robbins was he was never even committed to communism or social action. He had never read Marx or Lenin. He couldn't even understand dialectical materialism much less have a conversation about it. He was just a self-centered son of a bitch. Brilliant but self- centered. He got out of the army in 1943 by telling the world he was a homosexual then in 1953 he gave names to the committee because he didn't want the world to know he was a homosexual. I guess morality is a matter of timing.

Robbins only went to communist meetings to make connections; to further his career. Hell, he would have joined the Girl Scouts if they let him choreograph a number. He was so weak. And they go after the weak ones you know. He named us to save himself – because he thought we would survive it all.

That time in America can't be forgotten because it was the subtlest and most insidious of all exterminations.

They said they were trying to eradicate the communists but communist equaled liberal and liberal equaled Jew. And if you were a Jewish writer or a director you had influence. Your thoughts got out to the general public. They weren't going after the little tailors or the kosher butchers because their thoughts never went farther then their front counters. They wanted the artists.

That committee of lily-white Protestants marched us in front their firing squad of fear and pulled the trigger on our lives and our work. It was an intellectual final solution to eliminate thought; they couldn't kill our bodies – they had done a damn fine job of that already – so they decided to obliterate our minds. And they targeted Jewish minds. Yes, they did.

Look at Lucille Ball – dear, darling Lucy who I adored. She was my friend. She and I drank each other under the table at MGM. She had opinions. She had thoughts. She knew what was going on. They found her Communist Registration card from the 1936 Election. She had signed it. She admitted she did it. They had her signature on the card and they called her in front of the Committee they said, "What is the meaning of this, Miss Ball and she said, "Oh, I signed it to please my grandfather" and they said, "Well, of course you did. Then there's no problem. Go back to work and have a wonderful life. Live and prosper." And that was the end of it. She could have called her show *I Love Lenin* and they would have forgiven her. And they did forgive her. Her ordeal started on a Monday and it was all over on Friday. But not a Jaffe or Chodorov or a Berman. Or a Phillip Loeb.

You wanted to hear about Phil Loeb? You got it. Phil was the brightest, most intelligent, kindest, funniest human being I ever met on this earth. Everybody loved Molly's husband Jake from *The Goldbergs* because they could see his goodness shine through – the whole country could see it - through a twelve inch television screen.

He lived his life practicing the greatest principal of America – that all people were created equal and should be treated that way. Even actors.  Outrageous! Do you know what his "Un-American activities" were? He was fighting for black actors to be able to use the same stage door as white actors, he was fighting for equal pay for men and women, paid rehearsal time, hot running water in dressing rooms. Horrible! Despicable!

So the Committee subpoenaed him and they blacklisted him and they destroyed him and then all of America sat back and said, "Of course he shouldn't work. He's evil. He's the Jewish devil!" And the man lost everything. And Kate and I took him in and he lived with us. We cared for him. We fed him and we clothed him and then we watched him disintegrate.

So one morning, Kate made him breakfast, he put on his coat, he said bye-bye, checked into the Taft Hotel and jumped out the window.

You want to talk about your stars on the sidewalk? How about when they're broke and broken and covered with blood? How about when the only place they have left to turn is an eighteenth story window? The House Un-American Activities Committee. What a joke. That was no committee; that was an inquisition. That was no investigation, that was a massacre! And they killed him. They killed my friend. THEY MURDERED HIM! And you know who was next on their hit list? ME! They were coming after ME! ME! And I was TERRIFIED! Is that what you wanted to hear? Is that what you came after? Good! You got what wanted. This interview is over!

*(He slams the bathroom door after he exits. Blackout)*

**End of Act One**

# ACT TWO

*(The time: fifteen minutes later.)*

*(The **ARTIST** re-enters with a towel covering his head.
He's very Shakespearean as he lifts it off his face.)*

**THE ARTIST.** I had a dream last night. I dreamed I was a
baked potato. I was slit from my chin to my pupik. I
was all steamy and covered with butter. And I was deli-
cious.

*(taking his towel off as he stares at the interviewer)*

I'm glad you stayed. I apologize. I'm sorry. I get upset
when I talk about Phil. I loved him. One night Kate
and I were having dinner and we had so much food.
She called Phil and said, "Philly, get over here right
now. No! Don't change. Come right now before the
food gets cold." And a few minutes later, the elevator door opened, Phil walked in, I took his coat and
he was standing there stark naked. We sat down for
dinner and nobody said a word about it. Just before
he left I said, "Philly, your fly is open." A few days later
he moved in. And I miss him.

*(A beat)*

You heard he died of an overdose? You're asking an
actor for the truth? Pills? Windows? What difference
does it make? He died of a sickness called the blacklist. And do you want to hear something funny? Three
days after he killed himself, the committee cleared
his name. Wasn't that nice of them? His death made
headlines, but his innocence never even made it
to page ten. You can tell me your name now. We're
having a relationship. Arthur? But you're so young,
you're a baby. Arthur, I have frozen food older than
you. It's hard to describe the climate of fear we all
lived in then.

Did you ever hear of a writer named Ring Lardner, Jr? He was a wonderful writer. He won the Oscar for the screenplay of *Woman of the Year*. You've heard of the Hollywood Ten? He was Number Four. He was also my dear, dear friend. He was called to testify before the committee and the committee chairman, a Representative Thomas asked Ring if he could name names. Ring said, "Yes, sir. I could name names. But I'd hate myself in the morning."

So Chairman Thomas thanked him for his testimony, cited him for "Contempt of Congress" and locked him up in a federal prison for a year. Three months into his sentence, guess who Ring's cellmate was? Chairman Thomas. He'd been sent up for payroll fraud; a real crime, not a made up one. And when they released him a year later, he realized his sentence was just beginning. Now strike that elegant pose again, Arthur. We have work to do.

Who named me to the committee? Martin Berkeley! He named me and a hundred and sixty two others. He was the Babe Ruth of stool pigeons. And you want to know something funny? If you put a gun to my head, I couldn't tell you who Martin Berkeley was. But still, a lovely invitation to a lovely party arrived. I was coming out of my building one day and there was a guy standing across the street. He saw me and his face lit up. He ran over to me and said, "You're Zero Mostel!" I said yes. He said, "Could I please have your autograph?" I said, "Certainly." I signed the paper and started to hand it back to him. He said, "Better you should keep it."

*(mimics opening a paper and looking at it)*

Could I please appear before the House Un-American Activities Committee on August 15, 1955? Of course! What an honor. An invitation I couldn't refuse. My lawyer kept getting a postponement thinking it would all go away. But it didn't. He told me that the committee had agreed that I wouldn't be asked to name names. That was a relief. So six weeks after Phil killed himself, October 15, 1955, I walked into the committee hearing room…

*(SFX: an audience mumbling. The stage lights go to black and a stark white light comes up next to the desk where he will testify.)*

There were glaring white lights everywhere and television cameras at every angle. I thought, "This is wonderful, the first time I've been on television in years."

*(SFX: Gavel pounding. He crosses the stage and sits on a stool facing the audience. The lights change again as if he is there.)*

**THE ARTIST.** Good morning, gentlemen.

**INVESTIGATOR.** *(V.O.)* State your name please.

**THE ARTIST.** My name? I would have thought you would have known that already.

**INVESTIGATOR.** *(V.O.)* For the record.

**THE ARTIST.** Oh, for the record? For the record my name is Samuel Joel Mostel. M-O-S-T-E-L.

**INVESTIGATOR.** Isn't Zero your given name?

**THE ARTIST.** No sir, Zero is a nickname. It represents the amount of money I've been making over the last few years…since your investigation began.

**INVESTIGATOR.** Is that meant to be funny?

**THE ARTIST.** Yes, it is. You see I make my living as a comedian. That was humor.

**INVESTIGATOR.** This is no place for jokes.

**THE ARTIST.** No, of course not. I apologize. I will try to answer your questions completely and seriously. Go ahead. What do you want to know?

**INVESTIGATOR.** Are you a communist?

**THE ARTIST.** Well, you certainly don't beat around the borscht belt, do you? No, I am not a communist.

**INVESTIGATOR.** Are you in favor of the violent overthrow of the government?

**THE ARTIST.** *(thinking about it)* Well, sir, as our fourth president, James Madison, for whom they named a lovely hotel on Collins Avenue in Miami Beach once said, "I believe there are more instances of the abridgment of the freedom of the people by silent and gradual encroachments by those in power rather than by violent and sudden usurpations." No, I don't think he was a Democrat, sir. I think he was a member of your party *(under his breath)* the Whigs.

**INVESTIGATOR.** Mr. Martin Berkley has testified that you attended a meeting of the Communist party in Hollywood in 1938.

**THE ARTIST.** Absolutely not.

**IVESTIGATOR.** You're sure?

**THE ARTIST.** I'm positive. I didn't get to Hollywood until 1942. I ate my last orange in 1943. I was signed to a contract at Twentieth Century Fox – or was it Eighteenth Century Fox?

**INVESTIGATOR.** Who else was at the meeting?

**THE ARTIST.** Sir, if I was not at the meeting, how could I tell you who else was at the meeting? Why don't you ask Mr. Berkley?

**INVESTIGATOR.** Mr. Mostel, hostile witnesses are not…

**THE ARTIST.** I'm not being a hostile witness; I swear I wasn't in Hollywood until 1942. Did you ever see *Du Barry Was A Lady?*

**INVESTIGATOR.** I did.

**THE ARTIST.** You did? You're the one. Well, we didn't start shooting that picture until the spring of 1942. Maybe if you could tell me where I met this man, Mr. Berkeley?

**INVESTIGATOR.** At Lionel Stander's house.

**THE ARTIST.** Ah. Well, now it makes sense. I've never been to Lionel Stander's house. And I assure you that I don't know anyone named "Berkeley" unless he changed his name from Berkowitz.

**INVESTIGATOR.** Have you heard of an Organization called American Youth for Democracy?

**THE ARTIST.** Yes, sir. In fact, I performed a benefit for that organization in 1946 – the year my first son, Joshua, was born. Hi Joshie, Daddy's on television.

**INVESTIGATOR.** Did you know it was a communist front organization?

**THE ARTIST.** How could I? Your committee didn't declare it a communist front organization until five years later – until 1951.

**INVESTIGATOR.** Were you ever a member of the Communist party?

**THE ARTIST.** Funny, I thought you'd ask me that. On the advice of my lawyer I will not answer that question based on constitutional liberties which I hear are granted to every individual in this land and which I'm sure this committee does not question. Do you? I will say I gave my services as a comedian to the American Youth for Democracy. I also gave it to organizations…

**INVESTIGATOR.** Did you know a man named Ivan Black?

**THE ARTIST.** Of course I knew Ivan Black. He was my press agent. He gave me my nickname.

**INVESTIGATOR.** Was he a Communist?

*(He reacts to the question he had been promised he wouldn't be asked. After a moment…)*

**THE ARTIST.** I will not speak about any other individuals – I will only speak about myself.

**INVESTIAGTOR.** Mr. Mostel, how do you feel about using your talents to raise money for communists?

**THE ARTIST.** That's like asking, "When did you stop beating your wife?" You know, I also appeared at benefits for cancer, heart disease and a host of other favorites. If I appeared at a benefit it was to be an entertainer, to make people laugh – to do my imitation of a butterfly at rest.

**INVESTIGATOR.** Is your imitation of a butterfly at rest funny?

**THE ARTIST.** On that - I'll take the fifth!

*(The lights restore)*

Next day in the papers: "Mostel Takes The Fifth." And that was the end of it. The whole thing was so stupid. Why were they going after actors? Why were they targeting actors? What did they think we were doing – giving acting secrets to the enemy? Ten years in limbo. Ten years of working in toilets. Ten years of getting paid half of what I had been promised. Ten years of Kate having to work to make ends meet because the government forbid me to make people laugh.

But they couldn't take a brush out of my hand. I didn't need anyone's permission to paint. And so I painted. And I kept creating here. You can prevent a man from selling his creations but you can't stop creation itself. Only death can stop that. And we all know that death is nature's way of telling you to slow down.

*(The phone rings again. He slowly turns to it as though he might kill it. He rises, stalks it, answers it and screams into the receiver.)*

Temple Emmanuel! *(then)* I will not go all the way up to Zabar's for sour cream. Sour cream is sour cream. It's cream and it's sour. I will get it from Gristede's and you will like it.

*(He hangs up without commenting)*

I spent two whole years here in this studio and then I got an offer as good as gold. It was a new play called *As Good As Gold*. And it was going to Broadway. Except it only got to New Haven. My friend Ring Lardner summed up the play beautifully. He said, "This is the worst fucking play I ever saw." The critics weren't as kind. We closed at intermission. The producers abandoned us. Just left us in New Haven. I told Kate, "We'll be stranded here forever." She said, "Look, the Jews got out of Egypt, we'll get out of New Haven." I never thought I'd say it. But doing that play woke something up in me. It made me want to be an actor again. I wanted to be performing. I wanted to stand up and say that they hadn't knocked me down. They hadn't knocked us down. So a bunch of us who had been blacklisted got together and gave ourselves a second chance. Burgess Meredith – I LOVE YOU BUZZ MEREDITH! He found this little tenement on the Lower East Side and he turned it into a theatre. You put up two more lights; you would have blown every circuit to Chinatown.

We put on *Ulysses in Nighttown*. Buzz cast me as Leopold Bloom. James Joyce. What staggering language. You know, when I was a kid I used to read *Ulysses* under the covers at night because I heard it was dirty. But Joyce can't be read, he has to be spoken aloud. In rehearsal, I would get so caught up in the language and poetry of the text that I would scream out the lines at the top of my lungs and that little tenement would shake to its very foundation. When that happened, Burgess would say, "Hold on to your tits, everybody! It's Zero Hour!" And the world made its way down to that tenement and up those shaky stairs. And we could feel the change – we could feel the cosmic consciousness of anger that had welled up in the six years since Joe Welch said to McCarthy – "Have you no shame? Have you no decency?"

You know, I changed my mind about your jacket. It's not so bad. But now the light has changed. The light always changes. So comes the expression "I see you in a different light."

You see me in a different light too? Who asked you? I told you this is my interview and I'll ask the questions. So, the next question; guess who called me? Why don't I just tell you because you'll never guess. David Merrick - the greatest producer and the meanest son-of-a-bitch in the history of the American theatre. And he wanted me to star in a new play - on Broadway. To star! The curse was broken.

A new play called *The Good Soup* being produced by David Merrick. I told him I wanted $1,000 week. He said, "Yes." I told him I wanted billing over the title. He said yes. I told him I wanted a car to take me to and from the theatre. He said yes. I said, "I want the title of the play changed." He said, "No." I said "You got a deal."

Everything was back on track. Rehearsals were going well. I didn't even mind that my car hadn't shown up to take me home one day. I could afford a cab. I could afford anything I wanted.

*(He steps downstage, calling a cab:)*

"Taxi! Taxi! 86th and Central Park West."

I was getting out of the cab in front of my apartment. There had been a storm and the sleet and the ice were terrible that day. I had just closed the door to the cab after giving the driver a very generous tip, when I looked up to see the M-86 crosstown bus careening toward me at 50 miles an hour. The driver had lost control on the ice and the bus was coming at me sideways. I could see the looks on the faces of the people in the window, helpless - horrified. They knew as well as I did what was about to happen.

I tried to do a glissade á semblé over the hood of the cab. But only my right leg made it. My left leg got left behind. The bus connected. It crashed. It crushed me.

January 13, 1960. You don't forget a day like that when five tons of steel uses your left leg as a parking lot. And you know what's so funny, I didn't feel it as much as I heard it - the popping and crackling of the bone splintering inside my leg - the tearing of the flesh, the stripping of the muscles – the leg shattering like a peppermint stick snapping in the hands of an anxious child.

I listened to the symphony of the strangers around me, screaming at the sight of the blood running down my left leg, warming my left foot. I swooned to the concerto of sirens speeding to the gruesome scene to save me. Spinning red lights, red lights, red lights then a stark white light. The silhouette of a dozen faces looking down at me. Then came the ear-splitting whisper from the doctor's lips, "We're going to have to amputate. There's nothing else we can do." Then there was another voice – it was my own. "Doctor, I've had that leg since I was a boychick and I've grown very fond of it and I would really like to keep it." And then...fade to black.

When I woke up, I thought I had been dreaming – a grotesque dream. But the stark white light of the hospital room and the buzz of the albino nurses hovering over my bed like wingless angels convinced me that it was no dream. And so I looked down for my leg. And it was there. It was still there. It looked like raw liver - but it was there. And it was going to stay there.

And after the sixth operation, everyone was amazed that the doctor had been able to save my leg. He was so proud of his work he asked me to appear in front of forum of a hundred doctors in the New York area to show off my left leg so he could explain what he had done. Show off a little I think, but I said, "Of course. You saved my leg. I'll do whatever you want."

A few days later, they wheeled me into this surgical amphitheatre to total silence. I sat up on a gurney in the front of the room. The doctor said, "Please show us your leg." So I lifted my right pant leg. Not a scar. The place went crazy. They jumped on their chairs applauding and screaming - you never heard an ovation like that in your life.

Then when they quieted down, I said, "Oops" and I lifted my left pant leg. It took fifteen operations but I could walk. He had saved my leg. And once in a while, on a good day - I can even feel it. Not often. I have to walk with a cane but still, I don't use it on stage; or when I paint. Do you know, the bus driver came to visit me? He brought me ice cream. We became friends. Dear friends. And do you know what the great miracle of that horrible, life changing accident - it got me out of *The Good Soup*. What a piece of shit that was. How lucky I was to have been hit by that bus.

It got my name in the paper and so the great Broadway producer Leo Kerz read about me. He came to the hospital and he said, "Zee, I'm…"

My friends call me Zee – unless they're from England then they call me Zed. He said, "I'm doing a Broadway production of Eugene Ionesco's *Rhinoceros*." I said *(he does an animal noise)* He said, "I want you to star." I said *(He does an even bigger noise.)* And I thought Ionesco meets Mostel. The absurd leading the absurd.

Was it difficult becoming a rhinoceros every night? Arthur, one critic said he was amazed that at the beginning of the play I was so realistic as a human being. I went into Sardi's one night after the show. Two actors were talking to each other. They didn't see me. One said to the other, "You should see Mostel in this show. Without any makeup he turns himself into a roaring, bellowing wild animal." The other one said, "I've never seen him in a play where he didn't." You see, anybody can become a rhinoceros. A rhinoceros doesn't think. It just knocks down anything in its path to get what it wants. It's not about absurdity. It's about conformity. It's about not becoming a Berkeley or a Robbins.

It's about being true to yourself and not naming names. *Rhinoceros* is about staying true to your art and not becoming like everyone else. I'm an impression-istic painter, right? Wrong! I'm a Mostelitic painter. I paint like myself. I don't paint like, er…Paul Cezanne, a great painter known all over the world except Montana. Cezanne paints a mountain. And we say, "Goodness, look at it! Isn't it wonderful. What does it mean?" It means nothing. It's a description. The meaning comes from the emotion that it pulls up in you. How does a painting make you feel when you look at it? You see Rembrandt's "Descent From the Cross" – how can you feel anything but sad? You look at a Modigliani, how could you not giggle. You look at Picasso's "Guernica" – how can you not be angry at the foolishness of war? No, a painting is…a mystery. The mystery of creation wrapped up in a painting. A mystery! Why do we think we have to understand everything about everything? No, mystery is part of life and some things should remain unanswered. So what's your next question?

No, I wasn't the first choice for *A Funny Thing Happened on the Way to the Forum*. I was the third choice. I was the third choice for everything I've ever done but everyone else was working. The great Roman playwright Titus Maccius Plautus wrote it for Milton Berle. They were very close friends. But Milton wanted too many changes. So they offered it to Phil Silvers but he said it was Sergeant Bilko in a toga. So then they asked me. Choice three. I had worked with George Abbott back when the earth was cooling and he sent me the script and I never hated anything so much in my life.

It was god-awful. Besides, I had been invited to go to the Moscow Art Theatre and play *King Lear* in Russian. And I thought, between *Lear* in Russian and *Forum* in English, *Lear* would have more laughs. But Hal Prince, the genius, offered me four thousand dollars a week. How do you turn down four thousand dollars a week? Especially when you'd been making four thousand dollars a year. But it was Kate who convinced me to do *Forum*. She said, "My darling, if you don't do this show I'm going to stab you in the balls." How do you argue with logic like that? Then Hal the genius hired the other geniuses - Larry Gelbart and Burt Shevelove to do the book, Steve Sondheim to do the music and George Abbott to direct even though Abbott was a hundred and seventy five years old at the time. And he hired the greatest cast - Davy Burns – the funniest man on Broadway, my old friend Jack Gilford and ten of the most beautiful girls you ever saw in your life. We opened in Philadelphia. There it was – right on the marquee – "The funniest musical in the history of Broadway." And the people sat in their seats like they were watching *Death of a Salesman.* Two and a half hours without a laugh. Without a titter. So the boys went to work. Every day it was rewrite and rehearse it and play the new show.  Rewrite and rehearse it and play the new show. Eighteen hours a day of torment on top of torture.

Larry Gelbart came in to my dressing room one night and said, "You know, if they ever find Adolph Hitler alive, I hope he's out of town with a new musical."

We opened in Washington to the same reaction. After the first Wednesday matinee there was a knock on my dressing room door. "Come in." I saw them in the mirror. It was Hal Prince and George Abbott. I saw them and I knew something was up. You know what they say, "Where there's smoke, there's salmon." At first I hoped they'd come to fire me because I had a run of the play contract so they would have to pay me off and I could go to Moscow to do my *King Lear.* But the news was worse than that. Hal said they believed in the show. I said yes. He said they knew the show could be fixed. Yes? And they had just the man who could fix it. They wanted to bring in Jerry Robbins.

A morbid silence fell over the room - over my heart. Hal said, "Well?"

I said, "Do I have to shake his hand?" Hal said "No." I said, "Do I have to eat with him?" George said, "No." Hal said, "Will you work with him?" I said, "Of course I'll work with him. We of the left do not blacklist."

The next day, we arrived at the theatre for rehearsal. There sat George Abbott, Hal Prince and Jerry Robbins: See no evil, hear no evil and evil. George Abbott said, "Jerry wants to show you how to do this number" and he walked right out the door. You could have cut the tension with the whisker of a cantor's beard. I stood upstage, Jerry stood downstage. He said, "Good morning, Ladies and Gentlemen of the company, I'm Jerry Robbins!" There was a lovely round of welcoming applause for our savior. When it died down, I thought I should welcome him too.

*(steps downstage)*

"Hiya, Loose Lips. How ya been? Haven't seen you since 1953 when you gave all those names to the Committee. You haven't aged very well, Mr. Robbins. Sleeping poorly from a bad conscience? Did you say hello to Jack Gilford over there. Say hello to Jack. You remember Jack - whose wife's career you destroyed. No, don't apologize, Mr. Robbins. What do you have to apologize for? You're a hero. You saved America with your testimony. They'll give you a state funeral when you die. But you won't be able to be buried in hallowed ground, did you know that? Because the Torah says that informers can't be buried in sacred ground. Your soul is going to twist and turn forever in the limbo of your dishonor and your spirit will roam the earth for all eternity like a golem. Like a feared and hated golem."

*(then, all smiles)*

Now, shall we do the opening number?

And that new opening number changed everything. It turned out Robbins and I could work together. We could work together because we put the creation above our individual differences. Our blood was on the floor...but *Forum* was a smash.

*(suddenly irritated)*

Now, I hate when I hear that. I hate when I hear, "Oh Mostel, doesn't stick to the script." That's absurd. I've always said every word the author wrote. I never moved a comma. I might add something once in a while to enhance the moment...

So during *Forum*, what was so terrible with announcing the results of the Sonny Liston - Floyd Patterson fight? I gave it a Roman context. I said he knocked him out in round XII. Now, one night we were doing a performance in St. Louis – in the great 12,000 seat outdoor amphitheatre  in the park – on the Fourth of July – and there are – FIREWORKS! Every sentence I'm saying is punctuated with an explosion. Should I ignore it? I don't think so. So I grabbed my stomach and apologized for having a Mexican dinner before the show. Of course it wasn't in the script. But then there were EXPLOSIONS!

And if Harold Prince thought I was so outrageous and terrible in *Forum*, then why - answer me why - was I his third choice to play Tevye? I was! They asked Danny Kaye first, then they wanted Danny Thomas and then Dan Dailey, Chief Dan George - anybody as long as his name was Dan. The show had been kicking around for years. It was called Tevye, but the problem with the show was that it was only about the character - that one character and the family. And I told them it had to be about the whole village and what was happening to the entire Jewish community. Sure, we could tell the story about one man, but there had to be a larger picture - a bigger world view. And to be honest, I didn't think it was going to be anything.

The creators wanted to make it so un-Jewish. They said, "No beards! None of the men wear beards." And "Let's have pastel talis." "And no ztis-ztis." You know what that is - the tassels on a prayer shawl. They said, keep them under your costumes and I said no - the audience has to see them. They have to know who we are. They have to love who we are so they can hate what's being done to us. Maybe I didn't think the show was great but I thought the theme was important. It was about tradition.

And it's funny - years later when they opened the show in Tokyo, the producers were worried that it would bomb. But one of the critics wrote, "Do the people in America understand this show? It's so Japanese."

I'm going to say this for the record and you can quote me – but that little weasel is a genius. Because he used the writers as his palette and the actors as his paint and he created a magnificent canvas.

And on opening night, Jerry Robbins saved my life. My theatrical life. I got out of my car in front of the stage door of the Imperial on 46th Street and I looked up at the marquee and the name of the show and then my name even bigger above and I saw the stage door and I started to go in.

*(He mimes trying to open the door and can't. He tries again and fails. He's crying and collapses into the stage right chair.)*

I couldn't do it. I sat on the curb and cried. One song from the show kept going through my head…over and over…in my head. The song about Chava.

And everything was a blur. For me. Here I was, playing a man who disowns his daughter because she married outside the faith just as my parents had disowned me. My brothers wouldn't let me see my father before he died. But I had to see my mother. To make it right again. My mother was on her deathbed. I brought Josh to meet his grandmother for the first time. And she said, "No. NO!" Then she died. Tevye had no choice. He says, "If I bend that far, I will break." And yet I wanted my parents to bend that far and they couldn't. And that collision of life into art smashed into me in front of that stage door and once again left me crushed on a curb.

Then Robbins came out – all five feet four of him – and dragged me through that stage door, pulled me into the dressing room, threw me into my chair, turned my face to the mirror. He said, "If not you, who? If not now, when?" And that did it. For whatever reason, twenty years of guilt lifted from my shoulders and I knew I could go out onto that stage and be Tevye. But Robbins never knew when to shut up.

He said, "Tell me what I can say to you to make you go on that stage." I said, "Promise me. Promise me that when you make the movie of *Fiddler* that I will play Tevye." But it wasn't meant to be. It was like a death in family.

And if they'd have given the movie to him to direct, I know he would have given it to me. But no, the producers decided to let Norman Jewison direct because he was a devout and religious Ultra-Conservative Presbyterian. And then for Tevye, Jewison gave the part to Topo Gigio or whatever the hell his name was. Shameful. A terrible piece of miscasting. Who was going to play Lazar Wolf – Liberace? What did I think of the movie? It was the greatest Western ever made.

*(suddenly angry)*

Don't even mention *The Producers?* Doing *The Producers* could never make up for not doing *Fiddler.* I hate that movie. I look like a beached whale. And do you know what the great tragedy of my life is, Arthur? With 15 Broadway shows, 25 movies and 5,000 paintings left behind, you know how I'm going to be forever known? Ah yes, Mostel – he's "the fat guy from *The Producers*". I sound angry? That's because deep down inside I'm an angry man.

You see, anyone who's been excluded is angry. I've been excluded as a man, I've been excluded as an entertainer and I've been excluded as a Jew. I've had a thousand doors slammed in my face, but I stand on the other side of those closed doors and pound and scratch and scream saying, "Let me in! Mostel is here! Son of Israel and Cina! How can you exclude the life of the party?"

And then the door opens and I don't really want to go in. After Fiddler opened, we heard from the politicians again. No, it wasn't a subpoena, it was an invitation. "To Mr. and Mrs. Zero Mostel. President and Mrs. Lyndon Baines Johnson request the honor of your presence on August 16, 1965 to join them for a state dinner honoring the prime minister of Israel, the Honorable Levi Eshkol." From the blacklist to the White House in ten years. I showed Kate the invitation and she cried. She sat in that chair and she wept, heaving sobs. The thought of having to eat with Texans was too much for her.

But we went and as we entered the front door, I thought about my parents. I could feel them there with me. "Mama, Papa, look! Little Sammy made it to the White House. I'm having dinner with the President!" And I could hear them say, "Sammy, we're so proud of you." There was an empty seat at the table next to mine. Kate joked – she said it was for Elijah. But I knew who it was for. I could feel him there next to me. Right. And he was sitting there stark naked. And I was angry that Phil wasn't there. But I'm an angry man. Any man of contradictions is an angry man and that's me. I'm delicate and vulgar, self-centered and generous. Heavy in repose yet light on my feet. I'm angry. I have a voracious appetite yet can't help biting the hands that feed me. I am a spoiled child, Arthur of the *Times*, screaming in tantrums for the attention I crave. Look at me, look at me, look at me. And yet I'm a scared child afraid to come out into the light.

I'm angry that I have to leave here tomorrow, my studio, my sanctuary with the only real friends I have – my paints, my canvases and brushes to start rehearsals for my new play, for *The Merchant* tomorrow that will take me away from here. I'm angry that it will be a huge hit because my name is on it and once again I'll hear the prison bars of the theatre clang shut as it locks me up eight times a week.

What else am I angry about? I'm angry that our time together is done. Why? Because you've gotten your story and I've finished the painting - although a painting is never finished - just abandoned. Besides, now it's your turn to paint me. To put me into the light and give back what I gave you. Some of it will be pretty, some ugly but it will be me. I thought I would hate this but I have loved spending every minute with you. I want to thank you for asking me to do it.

*(pause)*

I was your third choice? You're funny!

*(The lights begin to fade as the music swells. He is about to put his brush down, but then* **THE ARTIST** *looks back at his subject.)*

Wait a minute. I just saw something else. Your ears! You know your ears look bigger when you're standing up than when you're sitting down. I've never seen anything like it.

*(The stage is now black....)*

**THE END**

# Also by
# Jim Brochu...

## The Last Session

## The Lady of the House

## Fat Chance

## Cookin' with Gus

## The Big Voice: God or Merman?

## The Lucky O'Learys

## A Wonderful Worldful
## of Christmas

Please visit our website **samuelfrench.com** for complete
descriptions and licensing information.

See what critics are saying about
# ZERO HOUR...

"Brochu has brought back to us the memory of a volcano that was thought to be extinct!" -Theodore Bikel

"Stages' *Zero Hour* channels Mostel's volatile presence. It's entertaining and consistently funny thanks to a steady stream of jokes that are potent and expertly delivered." –Everett Evans, *The Houston Chronicle* - Critics Choice

"*Zero Hour* is an impressive tour de force - a fitting tribute to an irreplaceable force of theatrical nature and a suitably outraged account of the cultural and political purges known as McCarthyism and their invidiously anti-Semitic effect. Mostel is peremptory, anarchic, outrageous, reflective, furious and very funny; Brochu peppering his script with the great comic's best quips. The amount of material and insight Brochu packs into the show is impressive, entertaining and salutary and his "Zero" is a moving tribute and a cautionary tale, well told." –Robert Hurwitt, *San Francisco Chronicle* - Critics Choice

"*Zero Hour* captures Mostel's rich contradictions in a loving but unvarnished homage as entertaining as the man himself. Jim Brochu seems almost fatefully destined to play Mostel. Brochu reintroduces us to the funny, fantastically contrary Mostel in all his biting intelligence and imperfection." –F. Kathleen Foley, *Los Angeles Times* – Critics Choice

"One person shows just don't get any better than this!"– Bob Anthony, *Washington Arts Review*

"*ZERO* SCORES A TEN. The show is extremely moving and informative. Brochu was a powerhouse, drawing the audience into a feverish dialogue, as though he was recounting his own life story, broken only by a brief comical interlude. The audience was at their feet even before Brochu appeared for his curtain call. I left the theatre in awe of the flawless, dynamic performance and highly recommend this show not be missed." – Jason Fisher, FiveMinutesToCurtain.com

"The initial, almost startling appearance of Jim Brochu in the role of Zero Mostel, so calls to mind a Hirschfeld caricature of the great comic actor that there is no need for a window of time during which the audience decides whether or not it will accept one distinctive actor playing another. Brochu creates a character that never fails to engage whether or not you know anything about Mostel. His performance is like a painting - a dab of bluster, a wash of insecurity and vibrant fields of talent and charisma applied to a sturdy canvas of humanity which create a rich portrait of the man." – Wenzel Jones, BACKSTAGE WEST

# THE BIG VOICE: GOD OR MERMAN?

Book by Jim Brochu
Music and Lyrics by Steve Schalchlin

*Musical / 2m / Simple Set / Piano Only*

In *The Big Voice,* Jim and Steve have musicalized their long term relationship and hilariously proved that theatre is as much a calling as the religion. This high energy, razzle-dazzle show chronicles the lives of a Baptist from Arkansas and a Catholic from Brooklyn who find eternal salvation in the temple of musical theatre. The show "traces the couple's meeting aboard a ship in the Atlantic Ocean, Steve's struggle with AIDS, the production of their hit Off-Broadway musical *The Last Session,* their separation and their reconciliation. It's a comedy about a 'gay marriage' between two men created by the couple themselves."

"Side-splitting! A hilarious and utterly enthralling evening of musical theater. Marvel at the romantic sweep of their songs. Here art is achieved with light hands, and the result is a triumphant and very touching song of praise to everyday love and the funky glories of the show business life."
– *The New York Times*

"The Big Voice" is unconventional and perhaps unlikely, but this story of a mismatched couple, musical comedy-style, is funny, touching and warmly endearing.
– *Variety*

# FAT CHANCE

## Jim Brochu

*Comedy / 2m, 3f / Interior*

Although Matisse Salinger is one of the most famous sculptors in the world, she has become a lonely, middle aged lady who hasn't left her house in years and speaks only to her longtime housekeeper, Aura Johnson, and her domineering mother and agent, Victoria Salinger. Without companionship, she turns her affection to food and does nothing but sculpt, sleep, watch TV and eat, eat, eat. Her world is shaken by the arrival of Alex Tyler, a handsome young man whom she hires as a model. Mattie and the young man fall in love and begin a beautiful May December romance until Mattie finds that she has been set up and the young model is not who he says he is. *Fat Chance* is a hilariously funny and sexy romantic comedy from the author of *Cookin' with Gus* and *The Lucky O'Learys.*

## COOKIN' WITH GUS

### Jim Brochu

*Comedy / 2m, 2f / Interior*

Gussie Richardson is a famous food columnist and cookbook author. Her agent comes to tell her she's been offered her own daily network television show. She wants to do it, but her husband Walter is dead set against it and Gussie discovers she has stage fright and can't open her mouth in front of a camera. Everybody tries to help her get over it . . . Walter through hypnotism, Bernie her agent by threats; and even wacky Gypsy Carmen from next door casts spells. Just when she thinks she's cured, the taping turns into a comic nightmare concluding in an all out food fight that almost ends the show and her marriage. *Cookin' with Gus* brings together four unlikely characters in a stew of hijinks and hilarity. Fun for the performers and a great evening for the audience.

# A WONDERFUL WORLD OF CHRISTMAS

Book by Jim Brochu
Music and Lyrics by Steven M. Schalchlin and Jim Brochu

*Christmas Play with Music/ 10m, 4f, some children, extras / 3 sets*

This classic for children of all ages is the story of Janie, a little girl Scrooge, and her brother Billy. When it looks like Billy's letter to Santa won't get to him on time, the Postmaster General of the North Pole magically appears and invites the kids to join him as he picks up last minute letters from all over the world. Climaxing with a surprise appearance by Santa, this show combines an original score with several traditional sing along favorites in a funny fantasy tour on Christmas eve. It is perfect for schools and large or small groups. (Running time: One hour.) Music published in script.

## THE LAST SESSION

Jim Brochu
Music and Lyrics by Steve Schalchlin
Additional Lyrics by John Bettis and Marie Cain

*Musical / 3m, 2f / Interior*
An Off Broadway sensation, The Last Session gathers a swing-
ing group in a recording studio to lay down a pop/gospel
idol's last album. With one exception, these are old friends
(including an ex wife) and the session is full of warmth, wit
and incredible music. The mix is somewhat altered by a
Bible thumping, homophobic gospel singer who is there to
replace the one no show of the regular back up singers. All
of them, even the sound mixer in the glass booth, are deeply
connected to Gideon yet are unaware that he plans to end
his struggle with AIDS after the session. Harmony is restored
through friendship and the power of music.

"Exquisite."
– *The New York Times*

"Very affecting.... Bright and funny."
– *N.Y. Post*

"Funny [with] charm and power."
– *N.Y. Daily News*

"The script is full of biting humor [and] the music is incredible.... Guaranteed to move you both musically and emotionally."
– MTV Online